SQUIRTLE™ Tinyturtle Pokémon	**08** **WARTORTLE**™ Turtle Pokémon	**09** **BLASTOISE**™ Shellfish Pokémon	**10** **CATERPIE**™ Worm Pokémon	**11** **METAPOD**™ Cocoon Pokémon	**12** **BUTTERFREE**™ Butterfly Pokémon	**13** **WEEDLE**™ Hairy Bug Pokémon
SPEAROW™ Tiny Bird Pokémon	**22** **FEAROW**™ Beak Pokémon	**23** **EKANS**™ Snake Pokémon	**24** **ARBOK**™ Cobra Pokémon	**25** **PIKACHU**™ Mouse Pokémon	**RAICHU**™ Mouse Pokémon	**27** **SANDSHREW**™ Mouse Pokémon
CLEFAIRY™ Fairy Pokémon	**36** **CLEFABLE**™ Fairy Pokémon	**37** **VULPIX**™ Fox Pokémon	**38** **NINETALES**™ Fox Pokémon	**39** **JIGGLYPUFF**™ Balloon Pokémon	**40** **WIGGLYTUFF**™ Balloon Pokémon	**41** **ZUBAT**™ Bat Pokémon
VENOMOTH™ Poisonmoth Pokémon	**50** **DIGLETT**™ Mole Pokémon	**51** **DIGTRIO**™ Mole Pokémon	**52** **MEOWTH**™ Scratchcat Pokémon	**53** **PERSIAN**™ Classy Cat Pokémon	**54** **PSYDUCK**™ Duck Pokémon	**55** **GOLDUCK**™ Duck Pokémon
ABRA™ PSI Pokémon	**64** **KADABRA**™ PSI Pokémon	**65** **ALAKAZAM**™ PSI Pokémon	**66** **MACHOP**™ Superpower Pokémon	**67** **MACHOKE**™ Superpower Pokémon	**68** **MACHAMP**™ Superpower Pokémon	**69** **BELLSPROUT**™ Flower Pokémon
PONYTA™ Fire Horse Pokémon	**78** **RAPIDASH**™ Fire Horse Pokémon	**79** **SLOWPOKE**™ Dopey Pokémon	**80** **SLOWBRO**™ Hermitcrab Pokémon	**81** **MAGNEMITE**™ Magnet Pokémon	**82** **MAGNETON**™ Magnet Pokémon	**83** **FARFETCH'D**™ Wild Duck Pokémon
CLOYSTER™ Bivalve Pokémon	**92** **GASTLY**™ Gas Pokémon	**93** **HAUNTER**™ Gas Pokémon	**94** **GENGAR**™ Shadow Pokémon	**95** **ONIX**™ Rock Snake Pokémon	**96** **DROWZEE**™ Hypnosis Pokémon	**97** **HYPNO**™ Hypnosis Pokémon
MAROWAK™ Bonekeeper Pokémon	**106** **HITMONLEE**™ Kicking Pokémon	**107** **HITMONCHAN**™ Punching Pokémon	**108** **LICKITUNG**™ Licking Pokémon	**109** **KOFFING**™ Poison Gas Pokémon	**110** **WEEZING**™ Poison Gas Pokémon	**111** **RHYHORN**™ Spikes Pokémon
SEAKING™ Goldfish Pokémon	**120** **STARYU**™ Starshape Pokémon	**121** **STARMIE**™ Mysterious Pokémon	**122** **MR. MIME**™ Barrier Pokémon	**123** **SCYTHER**™ Mantis Pokémon	**124** **JYNX**™ Humanshape Pokémon	**125** **ELECTABUZZ**™ Electric Pokémon

CONTENTS

Published by Pedigree Books Limited
The Old Rectory, Matford Lane, Exeter EX2 4PS. E-mail books@pedigreegroup.co.uk
Published in 2002

£6.99

MEET YOUR Pokémon PALS

Ash is a young Pokémon trainer who wants to win every battle and collect all the Pokémon and rise to the rank of a master trainer.

#151

MEW™
Aurora Pokémon

TYPE:	Psychic		
HEIGHT:	0.4m	**WEIGHT:**	40kg
ATTACKS:	Pound, Transform, Mega Punch, Metronome		
	Psychic, Ancient Power		
EVOLUTION:	None		

So rare that it is still said to be a mirage by many experts. Only a few people have seen it worldwide. Apparently, it appears only to those who are pure of heart and have a strong desire to see it. Its DNA is said to contain the genetic codes of all Pokémon, so it can use all kinds of techniques.

MEWTWO™ STRIKES BACK

In a hidden laboratory, the evil Giovanni's dedicated scientists had spent years trying to create a genetically enhanced clone of the legendary Pokémon, Mew. And now, after many failures, success was at hand! A clone began to grow in one of their tanks. It could think. It could feel, and very soon...

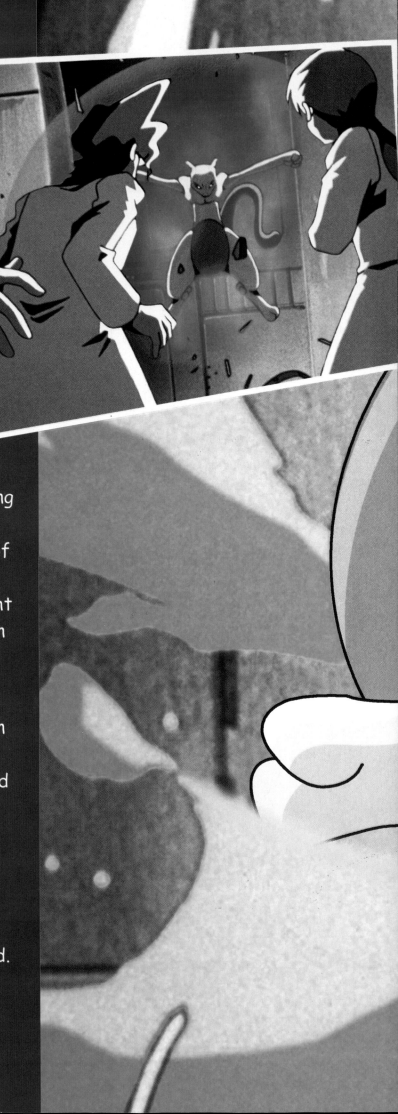

...it was born! "Doctor!" screamed one of the scientists, as the tank exploded, sending deadly glass shards across the laboratory. "Look at this!" The leader of the scientists, known only as The Professor, stared in wonder at the sight before him. A clone Pokémon of his own making...and it was alive!

"Aaaii...! It has awakened!" gasped another scientist, as the clone Pokémon opened its eyes for the first time, looking around at the destruction it had caused. Smiling triumphantly, The Professor ordered for Giovanni to be informed and brought to the lab – immediately!

Meanwhile, he addressed the clone. "Speak to us!" The Professor demanded. "Use your psychic powers!" The clone frowned deeply, confusion swirling around it its head. "Psychic powers?

"For ten years," The Professor revealed. "We struggled to create a super clone that would prove our theories...but you're the first specimen to survive!" He showed the clone an image. "That is Mew," he explained. "The rarest of all Pokémon. We used its DNA to create you – Mewtwo!"

"Mewtwo?" repeated the clone, as if it were its name. "But if I am only a copy of Mew...does that mean I'm nothing but Mew's shadow?" The Professor shook his head, explaining that the clone was greater than Mew, existing only through the power of human ingenuity!

Mewtwo felt a rising anger inside of him. "I am only the end result of your experiments?" it demanded. "What becomes of me now?!"

The Professor smiled coldly. "Our experiment is just beginning!" he crowed. "We can start on Mew-Three!" The disgust, anger and hatred he felt for the scientists boiled inside of Mewtwo!

His telekinetic powers grew stronger, aching to burst free! "Is this my purpose?" thought Mewtwo bitterly. "Am I just their laboratory specimen? THIS CANNOT BE MY DESTINY!"

Telekinetic energies of incredible power exploded from Mewtwo's mind! BOOOOOOOM! The laboratory was destroyed in an instant, as were most of the scientists!

 As the building collapsed around him, flames whipping at his coat, the badly injured The Professor watched in pride and admiration as Mewtwo levitated up into the smoked-filled air and out of the laboratory! "It was our dream to create the world's strongest Pokémon," he thought, moments before a second explosion obliterated the laboratory completely. "And we succeeded..."

Outside the wrecked laboratory, Mewtwo surveyed the destruction he had caused. "Behold my powers! I am the strongest Pokémon in the world!" Lost in his thoughts, Mewtwo was unaware of Giovanni's helicopter landing!

"Those fools thought you were a science experiment," announced Giovanni, alighting from the vehicle behind Mewtwo. "But I see you as a valuable partner. With your psychic powers and my resources, we can control the world!"

"I do not need your help for that, human!" hissed Mewtwo, who's hatred for humans still festered inside of him. Giovanni smiled. He told Mewtwo that, untrained, his powers could destroy the world! "Unless you learn how to control them," he said. "Trust me, and I'll show you how to become invincible!"

Taking Mewtwo to another laboratory, Giovanni dressed him in an exo-skeleton to focus his powers. Then he pitted him against various other powerful Pokémon! With his telekinetic powers, Mewtwo won every time! "Now I perceive my power," he declared, after many battles. "But what is my purpose?!"

Mewtwo was told that he was created to obey his master, Giovanni! "Humans may have created me," snarled Mewtwo. "But they will never enslave me!" And with that, he released a terrifying telekinetic blast that destroyed the exo-skeleton! KAAAA-BOOOOOM!

Flying away, Mewtwo had many questions. "Who am I? What is my reason for being? I will find my own purpose...and purge the planet of all who would oppose me – humans and Pokémon alike! The reign of Mewtwo will soon begin!"

Elsewhere, Ash, Misty and Brock were chilling out on grasslands above a coast. Suddenly, an older trainer appeared, challenging Ash to a Pokémon battle! "I choose you, Bulbasaur!" cried Ash, throwing a Poké ball, which burst open releasing Bulbasaur! "Ready when you are!" snorted Ash, as the older trainer released a Donphan to fight his battle!

Bulbasaur struck the Donphan down with a powerful Solar Beam! FAIHMMM!

The Trainer retaliated with his Machamp Pokémon, who threw Bulbasaur off his feet with a Seismic Toss attack! RRRRUUUMMMBBBLLLE! "Hmm," smiled Ash, throwing another Poké ball. "Then we'll go with – Squirtle!" Squirtle's Squirtle Bubble soon put paid to Machamp! BLUP! BLUP! BLUP!

"I can't believe it!" cried the older trainer, seeing Machamp flat out on the ground, unconscious. He threw three more Poké balls to release the rest of his Pokémon, Golem, Venonat and Pinsir! "Take this!" he snarled at Ash, as the Poké balls burst open. "I've got nothing to lose!"

"I choose you, Pikachu!" cried Ash, as Pikachu leapt onto his shoulder. "PIKA!" shouted Pikachu, and released a Thundershock so powerful, it knocked out all the older trainer's Pokémon! BZZZZZAAAAPP! They were down – and out! Ash had won the Pokémon battle! "Well, that sure was a shocking ending!" laughed Brock, as the older trainer headed off in disgrace.

On a hilltop overlooking the action, Team Rocket, Jesse, James and Meowth were spying on Ash and his friends. "Wow!" gasped James, impressed by what he had seen. "We've got to get our hands on that Pikachu!"

Also watching the Pokémon battle from his secret hideout on New Island, was Mewtwo himself! "I must bring those trainers and their Pokémon here," he decided, despatching a Dragonite to deliver an invitation to the children!

"Cool!" said Ash, when he read the invite. "We've been chosen to attend a special gathering hosted by the world's greatest Pokémon master at his palace on New Island! Let's go!"

Desperate to know what the Dragonite had delivered to Ash, Team Rocket ambushed it as it flew back to its master. Falling out of the dazed Dragonite's pouch was the invitation Ash had signed to say he would attend the gathering!

"Hmm," purred Jesse. "The world's greatest Pokémon master? I think we should go and meet him for ourselves!"

Beneath the seas below Mewtwo's palace on New Island, something stirred, Something that had been awoken by the noisy preparations Mewtwo was making to greet his guests. And that something...was Mew himself!

Reaching the ferry, Ash and friends were surprised to find that other Pokémon trainers had been invited to New Island! From nowhere, a freak storm, created by Mewtwo, sprang up, causing the ferry to be cancelled! To make matters worse, the local Nurse Joy had gone missing!

Some of the other trainers used their Pokémon to reach New Island, such as a trainer named Neesha and her Pokémon Dewgong, and Fergus, who's Gyardos was powerful enough to brave the storm! But Ash and his friends were stranded – Onix and Charizard, the only Pokémon they had who were strong enough to carry humans, were weak against water!

Moments later, team Rocket, disguised as Vikings, appeared and offered the friends a lift in their boat. A sudden wave struck the boat, washing away Jesse and James' disguises! "Those aren't Vikings!" gasped Brock, as the boat began to capsize! "It's Team Rocket!" But before they could react, the boat sank and everyone was thrown into the cruel, bitterly cold sea!

The waves pounding them, their lungs filling with water, Ash cried, "I choose you, Squirtle!" and Misty called upon Staryu, and the two Pokémon used their combined turtle and psychic powers to pull the friends through the sea!

For no reason, the storm quickly died down. Through the mist that stroked across the water Ash could make out an amazing sight. "It's

ME AND MY SHADOW!

Can you match up the Pokémon with their shadows? And which Pokémon is the only one with two shadows?

SQUIRTLE™

PIKACHU™

LEDIAN™

NOCTOWL™

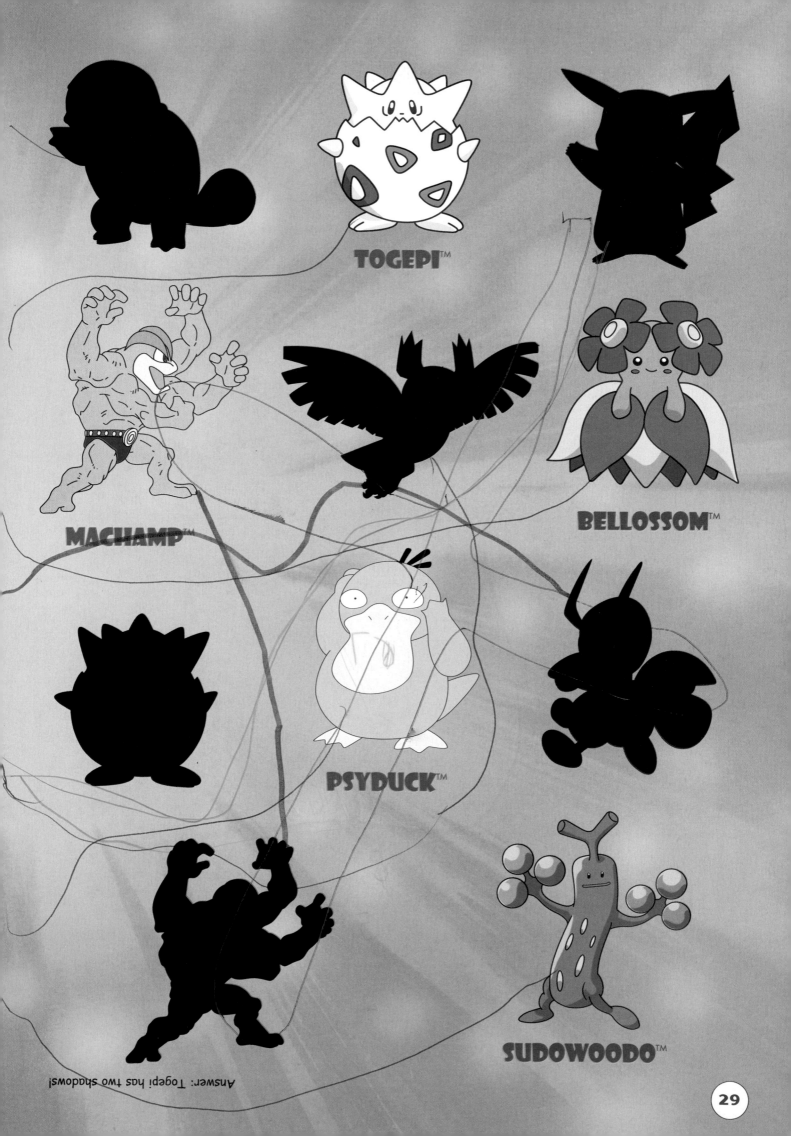

TOGEPI™

BELLOSSOM™

MACHAMP™

PSYDUCK™

SUDOWOODO™

Answer: Togepi has two shadows!

29

POKÉMON, POKÉMON EVERYWHERE

Oops! Brock might be a great Pokémon breeder, but he's accidentally allowed all his Pokémon to escape from their Poké Balls! Can you count how many Pokémon there are altogether, and how many of each type? Write your answers in the boxes below!

	CHARMANDER	7
	HORSEA	6
	SKARMONY	6
	SLUGMA	7
	FORRETRESS	5
	CATAPIE	4

Answers: There are 7 Charmander, 6 Horsea, 6 Skarmory, 8 Slugma, 5 Forretress and 4 of Catapie. There are 36 Pokémon altogether!

POKÉMON PURSUIT!

Can you help Pikachu reach Ash without running into the mean and nasty Meowth?! MEEOOOWW!!

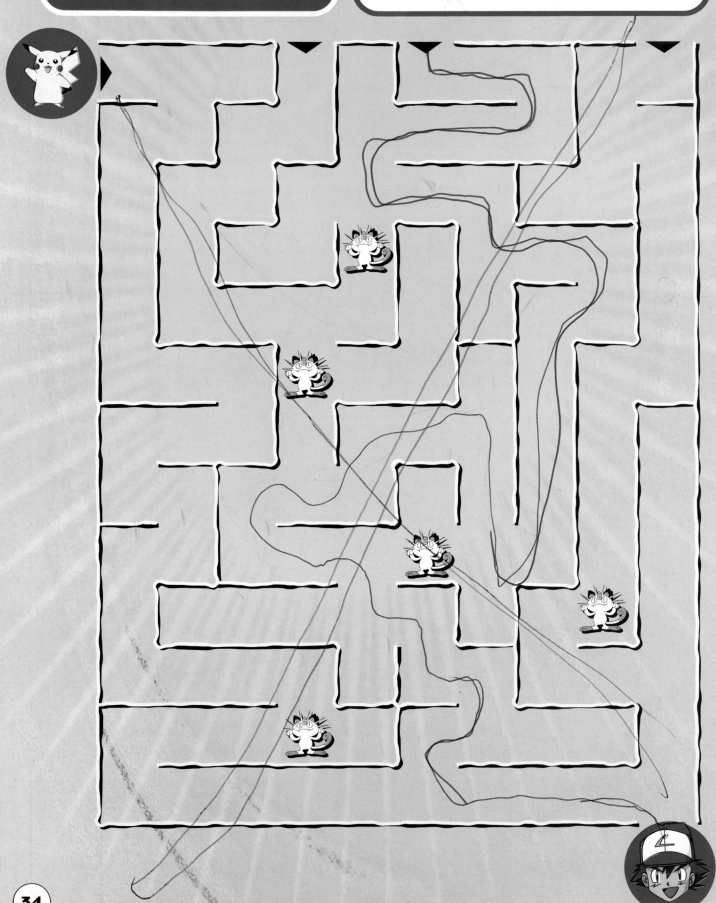

MEWTWO™ STRIKES BACK CHAPTER II

THE ULTIMATE TRAINER

Struggling against the turbulent waves that threatened to drown them, Ash, Brock, Misty and their Pokémon managed to reach the island, clambering up the wet rocks! At the gate of the palace, they were met by a mysterious young woman.

Showing the woman their invitation, they were admitted to New Island. "Hey! Aren't you that nurse who's missing?" asked Brock, referring to the missing Nurse Joy, but the woman denied this. "I have always dwelt on this island," she said.

Meanwhile, Mew had been attracted by the noise of giant rotors on top of the palace that were powering Mewtwo's machines hidden inside.

Mew wondered what was going on? "Mew!" he said, determined to find out!

The mysterious woman led the friends inside the palace. "Please, come this way," she said. "Now that you are here, all the trainers are present. My master awaits your arrival."

Inside a large room, they discovered Neesha and Fergus with their Pokémon, and another boy, Corey, who was petting his Pidgeot. "Aren't we going to wait for the others?" asked Misty.

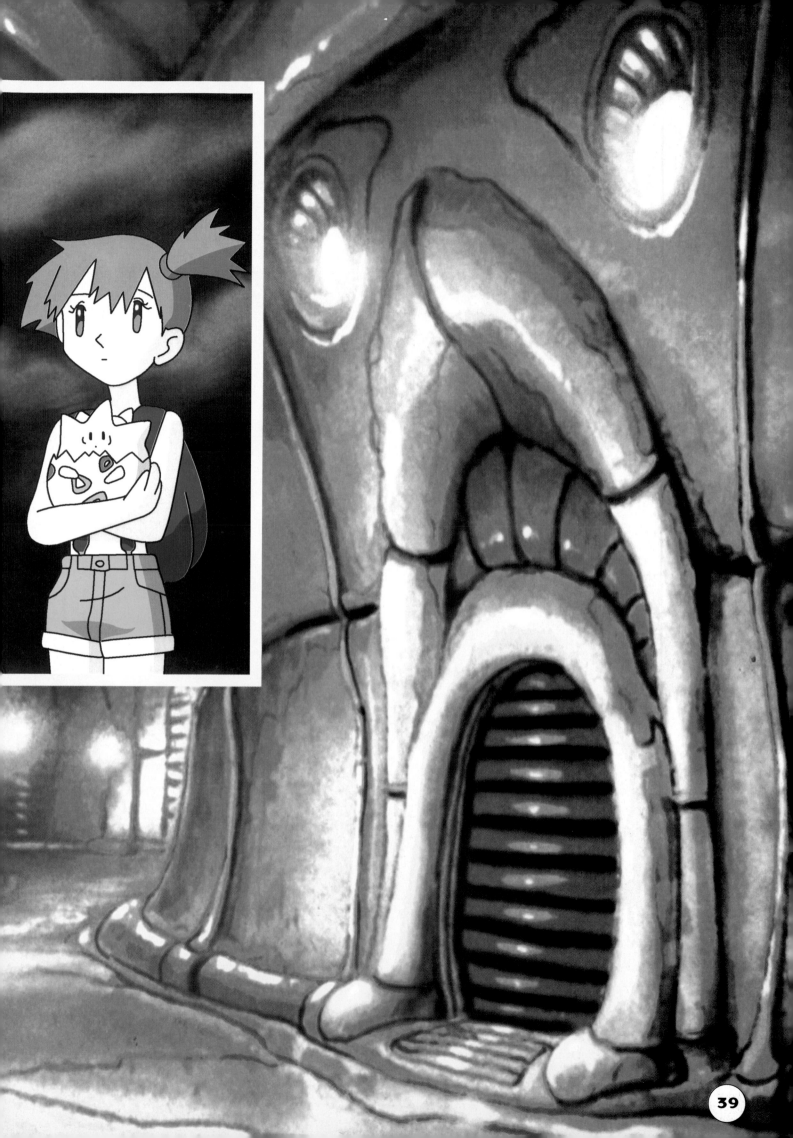

To their own disbelief, Team Rocket and Meowth had survived the deadly storm, too! Crawling up through a storm drain, they found themselves inside the palace – and wondered just where the heck they were!

Just then, Jessie thought she caught a glimpse of something hovering above their heads. It was Mew! But when she looked again, he had turned invisible and she couldn't see him. "Huh! Must have been my imagination!" she snorted, as they explored the palace.

Elsewhere, the trainers were introducing each other. "I decided to fly over here," Corey told them. "Hurricane winds are a breeze for Pidgeot!"

"These are my Pokémon," he said, gesturing to a group of other Pokémon. "Hey, guys, say hello!"

"You haven't met my Pokémon," said Neesha. "Over there!"

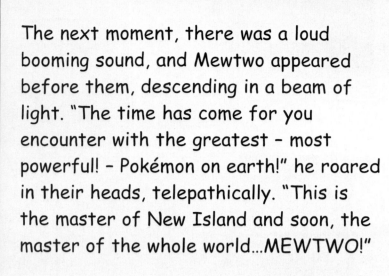

The next moment, there was a loud booming sound, and Mewtwo appeared before them, descending in a beam of light. "The time has come for you encounter with the greatest – most powerful! – Pokémon on earth!" he roared in their heads, telepathically. "This is the master of New Island and soon, the master of the whole world...MEWTWO!"

"Mew...Two?" gasped Ash. "A Pokémon can't be a Pokémon master!" Pikachu nodded furiously. "PIKA!" he agreed.

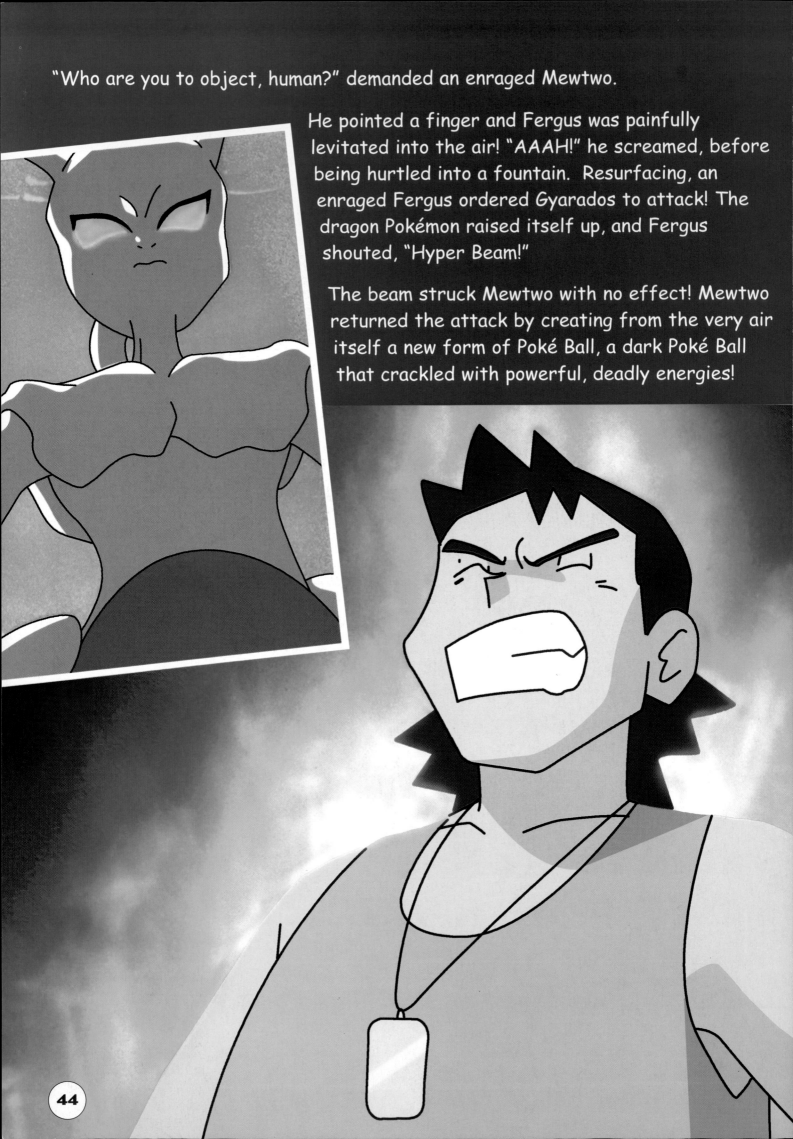

"Who are you to object, human?" demanded an enraged Mewtwo.

He pointed a finger and Fergus was painfully levitated into the air! "AAAH!" he screamed, before being hurtled into a fountain. Resurfacing, an enraged Fergus ordered Gyarados to attack! The dragon Pokémon raised itself up, and Fergus shouted, "Hyper Beam!"

The beam struck Mewtwo with no effect! Mewtwo returned the attack by creating from the very air itself a new form of Poké Ball, a dark Poké Ball that crackled with powerful, deadly energies!

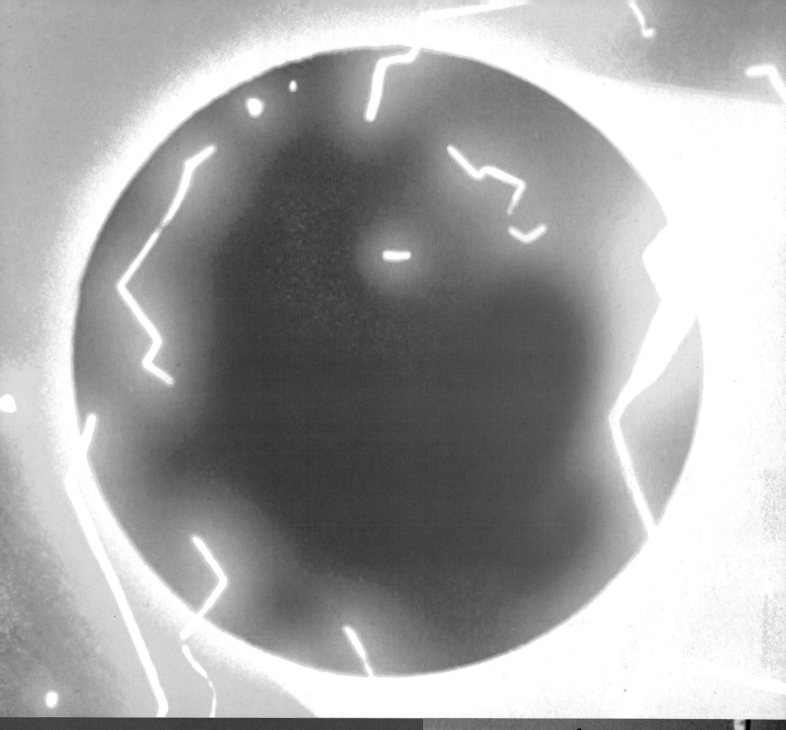

He threw it at Gyarados! The ball stuck home - and there was a terrible scream from Gyarados as the Poké Ball exploded, his insides freezing up from such an intense cold, he collapsed in unimaginable pain and agony!

Mewtwo then turned to the mysterious woman. He snapped his fingers and she collapsed in Brock's arms! Recovering, she revealed she was indeed the missing Nurse Joy, but…"Where am I?…" she asked.

Mewtwo's voice boomed inside their heads. "You have been under my control," he said, addressing Nurse Joy. "Your knowledge of Pokémon physiology proved useful t my plan. I am the new ruler of this world, the master of Pokémon and humans alike.

"No, you're not!" shouted Misty. "You're just a bully!" Pikachu snorted. "PIKA!" he growled in agreement.

Team Rocket had found their way inside Mewtwo's secret lab. It was filled with strange machines, and cylinders full of green life fluids. Floating inside the cylinders were fully-formed clones of Pokémon! "What is this place?" gasped Jessie, sitting down on a control panel, trying to make sense of it all.

By doing so, she accidentally switched on the machine! "This is a Pokémon replication system," a robotic voice boomed out. "System activated. "Pokémon based on genetic analysis...Pokémon DNA sampling sequence...now in progress."

The cloning machine detected poor Meowth and pulled him inside. "Hey, put me down!" he screamed.

Jessie and James pulled Meowth free of the machine, but it was too late! The machine had already begun the process of cloning Meowth! "A year ago," a human voice spoke. "We discovered a fossil of the legendary Pokémon...Mew! Giovanni insisted we create super-clone's from Mew's genetic material...we produced a Pokémon we called 'Mewtwo'. But it's anger is out of control! It's destroying our laboratory!"

"So this must be the lab," said James, unaware that Mew was listening in on the conversation. "But if Mewtwo destroyed it, somebody rebuilt it! But, who?"

If James had been with Ash and his friends, he would have already known the answer to that! Mewtwo revealed to the Pokémon trainers that he planned to kill all humans and ordinary Pokémon, since the Pokémon were little more than slaves – they disgraced themselves by serving humans!

Pikachu tried to stand up for his friends. "Pika! Pikapi!" he shouted. Mewtwo glared at him coldly. "So you say I am wrong – that you are not this human's servant, you are his friend?" He waved a hand and his telekinetic powers sent Pikachu hurtling through the air! Ash managed to grab Pikachu, just in time! "You are as pathetic as the rest!" hissed Mewtwo.

In the lab, Jessie screamed as the clones burst free of their life cylinders! The clones made their way to where Mewtwo was calling them!

"Like most Pokémon trainers, I, too, began with Charmander, Squirtle and Bulbasaur," Mewtwo's telepathic voice crowed. "But for their evolved forms, I used their genetic material...to clone even more powerful copies!"

To Ash's astonishment, the room converted into a giant stadium. "Of course!" gasped Ash, realising why Mewtwo had brought them to New Island. "Mewtwo planned this all along!"

The trainers attacked with their Pokémon, but Mewtwo's clones were too strong! One by one, they fell! First, Corey's Venusaur...!

...and then Neesha's Blastoise!

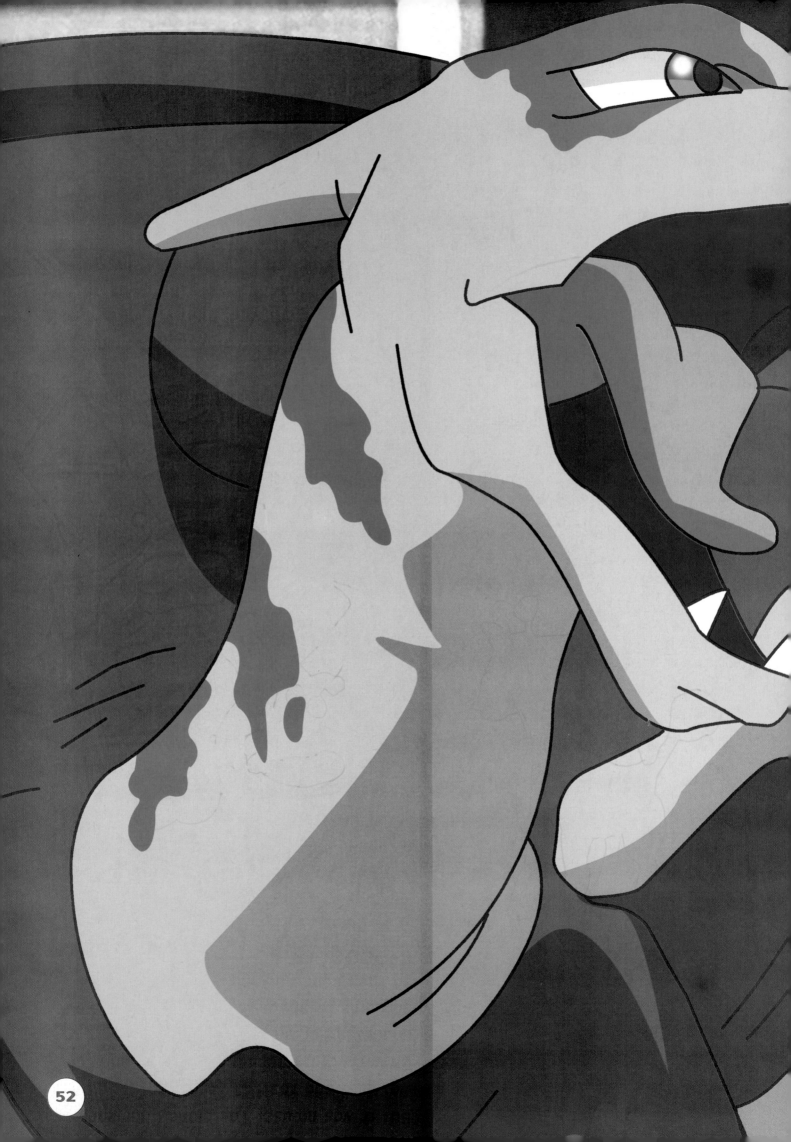

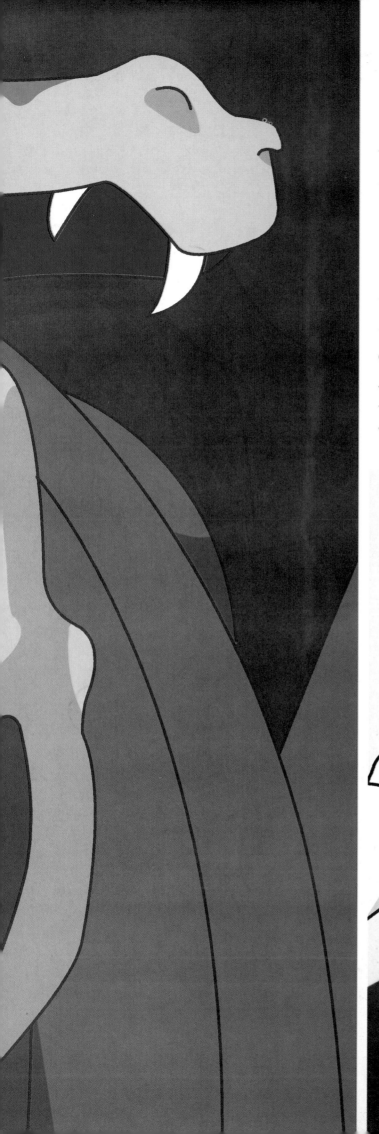

"I'm not giving up!" snarled Ash, grimly. He ordered Charizard to attack Mewtwo's own Charizard clone! "Use your speed – not your power," Ash shouted out instructions as the Charizards clashed in the air. "And we'll win!"

But it was no use! The clone Charizard was just too fast! It tore into Charizard, battering him, again, and again...and again...! "CHARIZARD!" screamed Ash, as Charizard dropped out to the ground, laying deathly still. "NOOOOOO!"

POKé DOTS

My Pokédex is suffering from a virus! Can you join the dots to find out who these Pokémon are and then put their names to the pictures? Afterwards you can colour in the pictures!

Answers: 1. GIRAFARIG, 2. MEWTWO, 3. SMEARGLE, 4. PHANPY, 5. GLIGAR, 6. SMOOCHUM.

Welldone

55

FOLLOWING IN MY FOOTSTEPS

Some of Ash's Pokémon have escaped from their Poké Balls and he's tracking them down! Can you help him match the footprints to the correct Pokémon?

1

A

POKÉMON POSTER

QUICK ON THE DRAW!

Wow! Feraligatr sure is rough, tough, mean and moody! No one messes with this Pokémon!
Copy his picture into the drawing grid and colour him in - but watch out! He bites! GRROOOWWLLL!!!

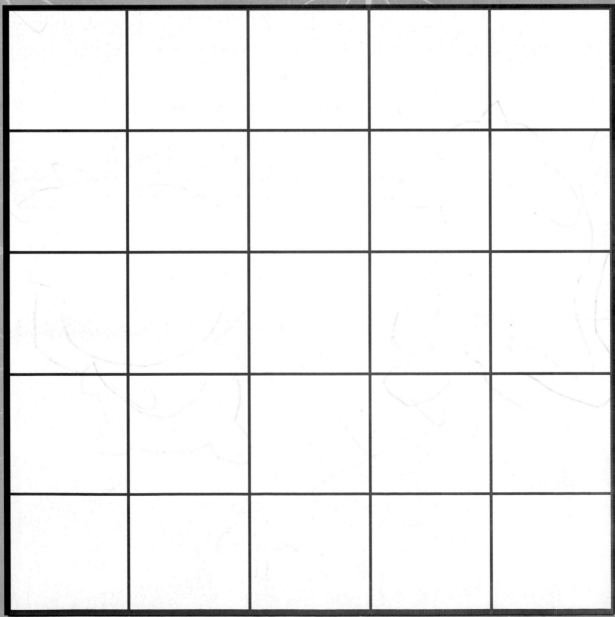

MEWTWO™ STRIKES BACK CHAPTER III

THE ULTIMATE POKÉ BALL

To Ash's relief, Charizard was still alive, but too weak to fight on! Mewtwo stretched out his arms, releasing specially designed Poké balls, which scooped up th Pokémon as their trainers watched on helplessly!

"I will extract their DNA to make copies for myself," announced Mewtwo. "Then my clones and I alone will remain safe on this island as I destroy the planet!"

"Everyone!" cried Ash to the few Pokémon left free as the Ultimate Poké Balls rained down on them. "Run! Don't let them get you!"

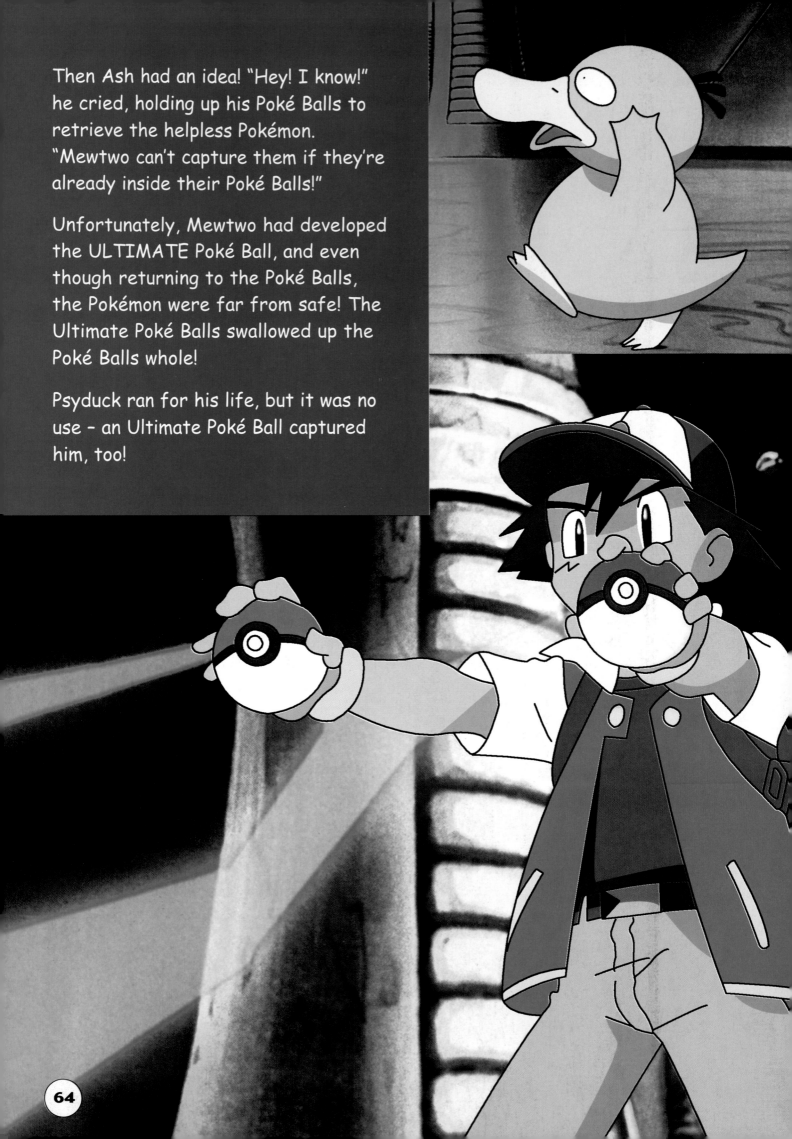

Then Ash had an idea! "Hey! I know!" he cried, holding up his Poké Balls to retrieve the helpless Pokémon. "Mewtwo can't capture them if they're already inside their Poké Balls!"

Unfortunately, Mewtwo had developed the ULTIMATE Poké Ball, and even though returning to the Poké Balls, the Pokémon were far from safe! The Ultimate Poké Balls swallowed up the Poké Balls whole!

Psyduck ran for his life, but it was no use – an Ultimate Poké Ball captured him, too!

Soon, only Pikachu remained free! He used his Electric Attack to fight off the Poké Balls! ZZZZZKKK! ZZZZZKK! "Keep running, Pikachu!" cried Ash, running after him through the palace to save him!

Pikachu leap from machine to machine, trying to escape, but in his haste he slipped, and fell onto a conveyor belt!

An Ultimate Poké Ball dropped down in front of the helpless Pikachu. The chase was over. Pikachu had been captured!

"STOP!" screamed a panicked Ash, leaping down after the Ultimate Poké Ball. "GIVE PIKACHU BACK!"

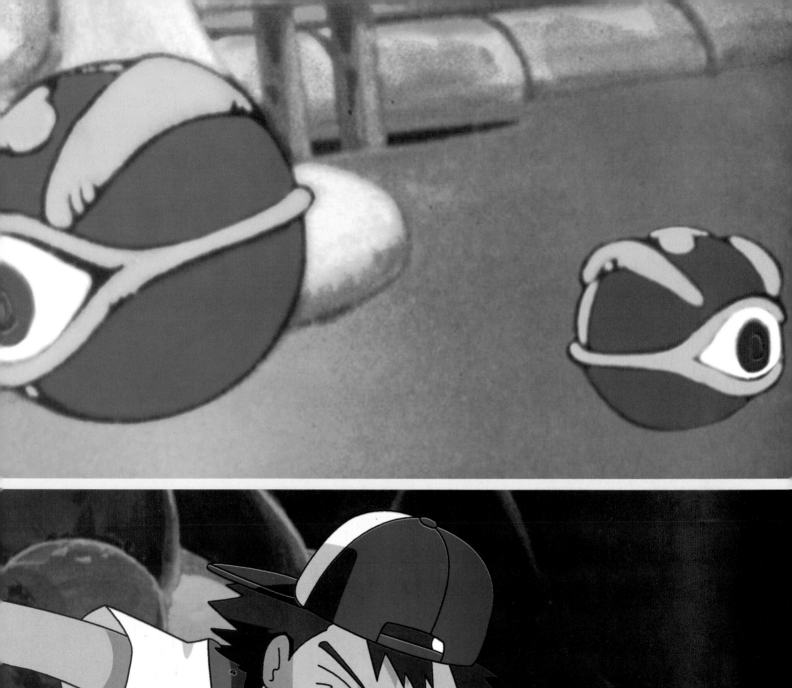

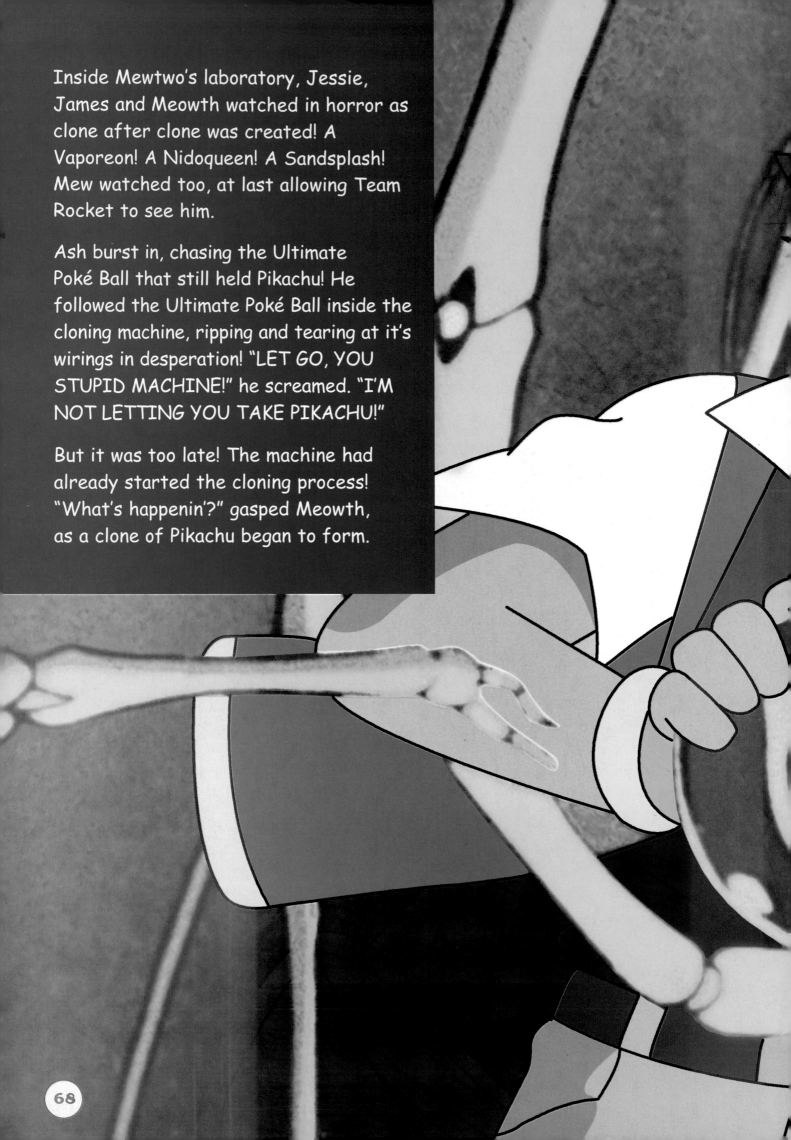

Inside Mewtwo's laboratory, Jessie, James and Meowth watched in horror as clone after clone was created! A Vaporeon! A Nidoqueen! A Sandsplash! Mew watched too, at last allowing Team Rocket to see him.

Ash burst in, chasing the Ultimate Poké Ball that still held Pikachu! He followed the Ultimate Poké Ball inside the cloning machine, ripping and tearing at it's wirings in desperation! "LET GO, YOU STUPID MACHINE!" he screamed. "I'M NOT LETTING YOU TAKE PIKACHU!"

But it was too late! The machine had already started the cloning process! "What's happenin'?" gasped Meowth, as a clone of Pikachu began to form.

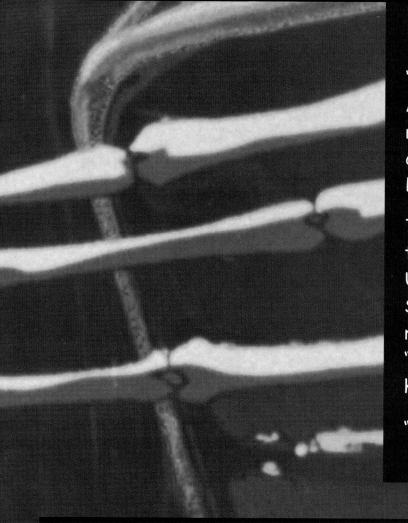

"It's not over 'til it's over!" screamed Ash, and with one last effort, he ripped out the machine's innards, causing it to explode! KAAA-BOOOOOM!

The cloning machine destroyed, all the Pokémon were released from the Ultimate Poké Balls! "Pikachu! Squirtle! Bulbasaur!" cried Ash in relief, giving them all a big hug. "You're all okay!" Pikachu giggled happily. "PIKACHU!" he cried.

"And now," growled Ash. "For Mewtwo...!"

Back at the Pokémon stadium, smoke from the explosion swirled in thickly to obscure Mewtwo's view. "What is going on?" he demanded, as dozens of Pokémon originals charged into the stadium. "You can't do this! I won't let you!"

Then, through the smoke, he discerned a figure strolling towards him in grim determination. It was Ash!

Behind him, followed more Pokémon. It was time...for a showdown!

"It's not gonna to end like this, Mewtwo," hissed Ash, as Mewtwo gathered his own forces of clone Pokémon. "We won't let it! CHARGE!"

Ash, his warrior heart pumping, attacked Mewtwo himself, throwing punch after punch...!

But a physical attack was impossible! Mewtwo simply formed a force field around himself, and didn't even feel Ash's desperate blows!

Pikachu and the other Pokémon watched on helplessly as Mewtwo focused his telekinetic powers on Ash, lifting him off the ground, and hurling him across the room! Ash would be crushed against the far wall!

Luckily, Mew appeared, and used his Bubble power to break Ash's fall! "Mew," hissed Mewtwo, creating deadly Ultimate Poké Balls with which to destroy his adversary. "So...we finally meet! I may have been cloned from your DNA, but I shall prove that Mewtwo is better than the original...superior to Mew!"

With that, he hurled the Ultimate Poké Balls, which a laughing Mew easily deflected with his powers, and they exploded harmlessly around him! Telepathically, he told Mewtwo that Mewtwo wouldn't prove anything if all he did was show off his powers! This enraged Mewtwo even more!

"Mew and Mewtwo?" gasped Misty, confused. "How can that be?" Ash grunted. "It's easy," he snorted. "Mewtwo was cloned from Mew!"

Ash listened as Mew told Mewtwo that special powers weren't important...real strength came from the heart!

"Very well," agreed Mewtwo. "I will block all of the Pokémon's special abilities – both originals and clones - with my psychic powers! NOW LET BATTLE BEGIN!"

GOTTA CATCH 'EM ALL

Play this cool game, either on your own or with a friend. You will need one dice and counters. You can start this game ANYWHERE on the board! Your task is to see who collects all the Pokémon first. (If your playing on your own, time yourself and see how long it takes!)

Take turns throwing the dice, and move the number of squares indicated. Each time to land on a Pokémon you haven't got tick their names off on the checklist. If you land on a Pokémon you already have, you miss that turn! The first person to collect all the Pokémon wins the game!

YAMNA

SUNFLORA

CHARMANDER

BULBASAUR

JIGGLYPUFF

WOOPER

MISDREAVUS

QUAGSIRE

ESPEON

PIDGEY

UMBREON

PSYDUCK

PIKACHU

SLOWKING

SQUIRTLE

ZUBAT

SCIZOR

BELLSPROUT

QWILFISH

GLOOM

GLIGAR

STEELIX

WOBBUFFET

SNUBBULL

PINECO

PINZER

CHANSEY

SLOWPOKE

81

WORDS UP!

Ha-ha! Look what we've done! We've used Giovanni's latest weapon to mix up all these stupid Pokémon names into the grid! Bet you can't find them!

```
C W H T W O E M S X C A R A P
A _ E N T A C O O L K T B F S
T S C R S X N F E G L O O M I
E A A E W I L O P R D Q E X W
R F T D X H J S Q U I R T L E
P A I N C C S Q V A W A I I B
I A S A M J U X W S I T G K G
E O K M I H U F T A G I M C R
W L S R C E R T Y B S C H U
P I W A R T O R T L E A W D M
W I Y H O A Z B U U M T N Y E
P D T C R K R A B B Y E F S R
R M A C H A M P A W Z I S X P J
Z U B A T E B R F R E T I U B
O D D I S H K O B R A O O A
A D K I J F U K I O O A G L C
X D R L E E Z O W T W E M F
A F M A B O U B G E L Q P S
A J R B D E E N S A M R I Z T
```

PARAS	ONIX	BULBASAUR	ODDISH
BUTTERFREE	GLOOM	ZUBAT	DODUO
MACHAMP	WARTORTLE	TENTACOOL	GRIMER
CATERPIE	CHARMANDER	SQUIRTLE	KRABBY
MEOWTH	RATICATE	ABRA	MEWTWO
PSYDUCK	PIKACHU	ARBOK	TOGEPI

WHO'S MY POKÉMON?

Can you follow the trail to find which Pokémon belongs to which person?

ASH

MISTY

BROCK

JESSIE

J

MEWTWO™

B

PINECO™

A

CHARMANDER™

M

QWILFISH™

MEWTWO™ STRIKES BACK CHAPTER IV

MEW™ VERSES MEWTWO™

"No!" cried Ash, trying to protect his Pokémon from harm. "You can't force Pokémon to fight! But Mewtwo's telepathic fury was fed into the Pokémon – originals and clones alike – and even though none of them wanted to fight, they found they had no choice!

"What's going on?" gasped Ash, as Pokémon fought Pokémon...to the death!

The stadium was filled with the roars and screams and cries of pain from both aggressive and injured Pokémon. The sight filled Ash and his friends with dread! Could it be possible that none of their Pokémon friends survived?!

The original Pokémon had to fight to protect themselves, the clones had to fight because Mewtwo was forcing them to! It was a no-win situation!

The original Psyduck refused to fight his clone, but the clone attacked him, anyway! Yet each time

he struck Psyduck, the clone cried out, "PSY?!", meaning "What have I done?!" because hurting Psyduck was like hurting himself! It was a terrible dilemma – no one knew what to do!

And worse was yet to come! Pikachu came face-to-face with the Pikachu clone, and the Pikachu clone was determined to prove who was the strongest!

"Pika..." said Pikachu, trying to express that he did not want to fight. The Pikachu clone ignored his pleas and attacked, first with a Thundershock and then with a Thunderwave! ZZZZZZKKK! ZZZZZZZZZKKK!

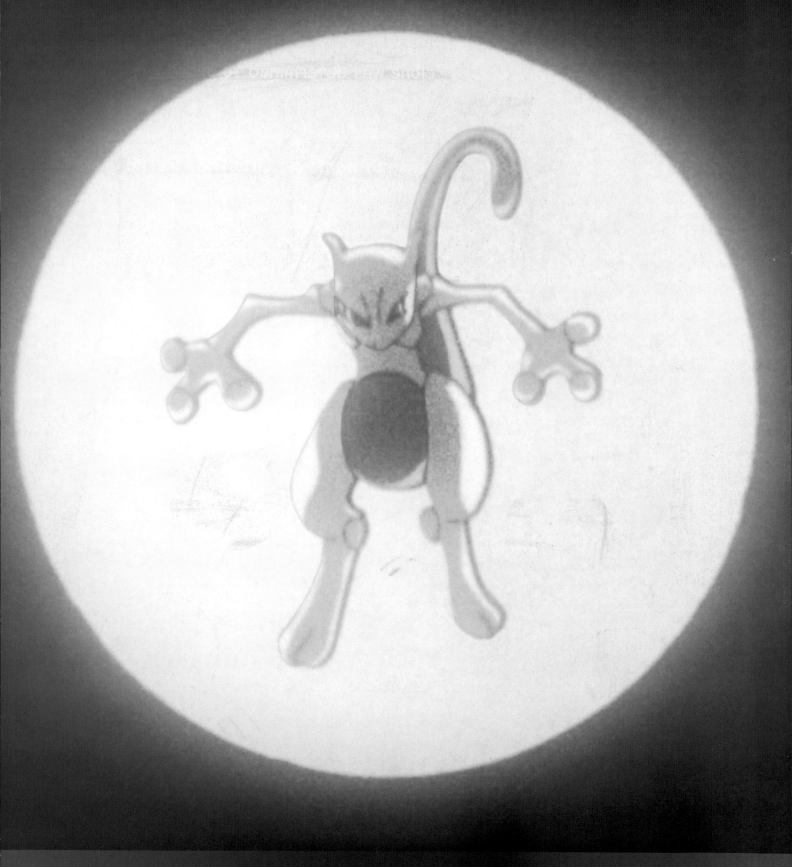

Pikachu crashed to the ground! And every time he rose, refusing to fight, he was struck down again! ZZZZZZZZKKKK! If the Pikachu clone didn't stop, Pikachu wouldn't survive!

In the air above the stadium, Mewtwo and Mew were blasting each other with incredible telepathic energies, that threatened to tear apart the entire palace! ZZZZZZZAAAAAPPP!

The Pokémon trainers were devastated to see such violence! "Pokémon aren't meant to fight...not like this..." cried Neesha. "What can come of it?" Corey shook his head sadly. "Nothing...but pain," he said. "Why can't Mewtwo understand that it's not right to force Pokémon to battle this way?"

Brock nodded. "They're all living creatures. All this proves is that fighting is wrong."

Even Jessie and James were upset at seeing all the fighting! "I was prepared for trouble...," sniffed James. "But not for this!" Jessie wiped back a tear. "Make that double...," she gulped. "For me!" They collapsed onto their knees and began to cry! "Now I can see how horrible fighting really is!" bawled James. Jessie agreed. "I'll promise never to fight again if you will!" she sobbed.

Even Meowth was moved! Yet he suddenly had troubles of his own! The Meowth clone appeared, ready to fight! Their claws came out...and both realised they might get badly hurt! "We don't have to fight," Meowth suggested, and the clone agreed.

"Maybe," it said. "If we started looking at what's the same about us instead of what's different, who knows? We could be friends!"

Ash watched as Pikachu received a pummelling from the Pikachu clone, but still he refused to strike back! "Pikachu!" he cried. "Wait for me!"

Too late! Weak from exhaustion, Pikachu collapsed onto the floor! The Pikachu clone prepare for the killing blow!

Horrified at the sight of his friend, battered, bruised and defenceless, Ash pleaded to the Pikachu clone! "Clone Pikachu or whatever you are!" he cried, tears swelling up in his eyes. "Please – stop!"

"STOP!" screamed Ash, running between Mewtwo and Mew, whose battle had descended to floor level. Unfortunately for Ash, he did so just as they both released energies of cataclysmic power – power that struck Ash down! ZZZZZKKKKKAAAADOOOOOM!!!!

He lay unmoving on the floor, as if his very lifeforce had left his body. Mewtwo was confused. Ash had risked his life for his Pokémon? Why???!!

Everyone stopped fighting, staring dumbly at the fallen Ash. Amid the silence, a heartbroken Pikachu desperately tried to revive his best friend with a Thundershock – ZZZZZKKK! - but it was no good. Ash...was gone!

Pikachu began to cry, his tears splashing on Ash's lifeless body. "Pika..." he sobbed. "Pikapi..."

The other Pokémon – originals and clones alike – moved by the love Pikachu had for Ash, began to cry, too. Their tears fell to the floor, forming rivulets that trickled towards Ash, touching him...

Pikachu gasped. Ash's body – twitched! Then – moved! Ash, straining, lifted up his head weakly. He was alive! Ash was ALIVE! "Pikapi!" cried Pikachu, overwhelmed with joy, leaping into Ash's arms for a loving hug!

It seemed that, united in grief, the Pokémons' heartfelt tears had miraculously brought Ash back to life!

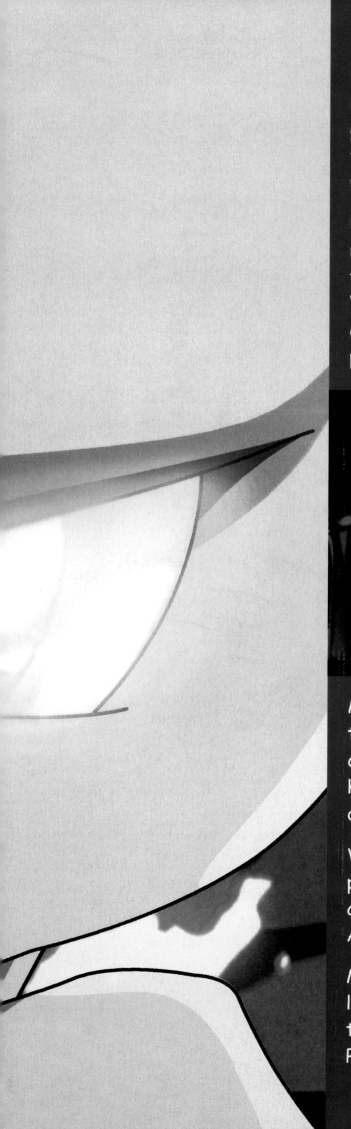

Misty, Brock and the other trainers were more than a little relieved! "Thank goodness..." sobbed Misty, and even Brock, turning away so that Misty couldn't see him, wiped away a tear...

Understanding began to form in Mewtwo's mind. "The human sacrificed himself...to save the Pokémon." Mew nodded. "Mew...!" he said. "I pitted them against each other," Mewtwo continued. "But not until now did I see the power they share deep inside."

Mewtwo felt strange. His heart...lighter. He thought he might even of felt...love. "The circumstances of one's birth are irrelevant," he said. It is what you do with your life that determines who you are."

With that, Mewtwo used his telekinetic powers to lift himself and the Pokémon clones into the air. "Mewtwo...," called out Ash. "Where are you going?"

Mewtwo called back. "Where my heart can learn what yours knows so well." And with that, he transported himself, Mew, and the Pokémon clones from New Island!

But before he left, he wiped clean the minds of the trainers and their Pokémons, making them forget everything that had happened. Then he returned them to the harbour, where the adventure had begun. Looking out to sea, Ash caught sight of Mew, winking at him, then he blinked, and Mew was gone!

Mewtwo had not forgotten Jessie, James and Meowth, either!

For their change of heart regarding fighting and violence, he transported them to a beautiful island where they could live out their days in pure, unadulterated happiness...

"I don't have a clue how we got here," sighed Jessie, happily, overlooking the view. "But who cares? This is PARADISE!" Meowth chuckled. "For once, a happy ending!"

POKéMON SCRAMBLED

Here are eight Pokémon and their names, scrambled up. But the names don't go with the Pokémon! Can you unscrambled the names, and then match the names to the right Pokémon?

In each scrambled name there is an extra letter – write down all the extra letters, unscramble them, and spell out the name of a missing Pokémon!

RSEORAHCSN

BUNULIBLS

RAMDUSEISVD

OOUFBEWBFT

OETRGXUEGR

PSKOWLEIO

ACPMHNMA

ASOAGDRAY

POKÉMON™

POSTER

126 MAGMAR™ Spitfire Pokémon	**127 PINSIR™** Stagbeetle Pokémon	**128 TAUROS™** Wild Bull Pokémon	**129 MAGICARP™** Fish Pokémon	**130 GYARADOS™** Atrocious Pokémon	**131 LAPRAS™** Transport Pokémon	**132 DITTO™** Transform Pokémon
140 KABUTO™ Shellfish Pokémon	**141 KABUTOPS™** Shellfish Pokémon	**142 AERODACTYL™** Fossil Pokémon	**143 SNORLAX™** Sleeping Pokémon	**144 ARTICUNO™** Freeze Pokémon	**145 ZAPDOS™** Electric Pokémon	**146 MOLTRES™** Flame Pokémon
154 MEGANIUM™ Herb Pokémon	**155 CYNDAQUIL™** Fire Mouse Pokémon	**156 QUILAVA™** Volcano Pokémon	**157 TYPHLOSION™** Volcano Pokémon	**158 TOTODILE™** Big Jaw Pokémon	**159 CROCONAW™** Big Jaw Pokémon	**160 FERALIGATR™** Big Jaw Pokémon
168 ARIADOS™ Long Leg Pokémon	**169 CROBAT™** Bat Pokémon	**170 CHINCHOU™** Angler Pokémon	**171 LANTURN™** Light Pokémon	**172 PICHU™** Tiny Mouse Pokémon	**173 CLEFFA™** Starshape Pokémon	**174 IGGLYBUFF™** Balloon Pokémon
182 BELLOSSOM™ Flower Pokémon	**183 MARILL™** Aquamouse Pokémon	**184 AZUMARILL™** Aquarabbit Pokémon	**185 SUDOWOODO™** Imitation Pokémon	**186 POLITOED™** Frog Pokémon	**187 HOPPIP™** Cottonweed Pokémon	**188 SKIPLOOM™** Cottonweed Pokémon
196 ESPEON™ Sun Pokémon	**197 UMBREON™** Moonlight Pokémon	**198 MURKROW™** Darkness Pokémon	**199 SLOWKING™** Royal Pokémon	**200 MISDREAVUS™** Screech Pokémon	**201 UNOWN™** Symbol Pokémon	**202 WOBBUFFET™** Patient Pokémon
210 GRANBULL™ Fairy Pokémon	**211 QWILFISH™** Balloon Pokémon	**212 SCIZOR™** Scissors Pokémon	**213 SHUCKLE™** Mold Pokémon	**214 HERACROSS™** Single Horn Pokémon	**215 SNEASEL™** harp Claw Pokémon	**216 TEDDIURSA™** Little Bear Pokémon
224 OCTILLERY™ Jet Pokémon	**225 DELIBIRD™** Delivery Pokémon	**226 MANTINE™** Kite Pokémon	**227 SKARMORY™** Armour Bird Pokémon	**228 HOUNDOUR™** Dark Pokémon	**229 HOUNDOOM™** Dark Pokémon	**230 KINGDRA™** Dragon Pokémon
238 SMOOCHUM™ Kiss Pokémon	**239 ELEKID™** Electric Pokémon	**240 MAGBY™** Live Coal Pokémon	**241 MILTANK™** Milk Cow Pokémon	**242 BLISSEY™** Happiness Pokémon	**243 RAIKOU™** Thunder Pokémon	**244 ENTEI™** Volcano Pokémon